The artwork was prepared with acrylic and colored pencil on hot-pressed watercolor paper.

Moonlight   Text copyright © 2003 by Cynthia Rylant   Illustrations copyright © 2003 by Melissa Sweet
Printed in the U.S.A. All rights reserved.   www.harperchildrens.com

Library of Congress Cataloging-in-Publication Data
Rylant, Cynthia.   Moonlight / by Cynthia Rylant; illustrated by Melissa Sweet.   p.   cm.
Summary: Moonlight the cat loves everything about Halloween, from pumpkins to children to candy.
ISBN 0-06-029711-5 — ISBN 0-06-029712-3 (lib. bdg.)   [1. Halloween—Fiction. 2. Cats—Fiction.]
I. Sweet, Melissa, ill. II. Title. PZ7.R982 Mo 2003   [E]—dc21   2001039511   CIP   AC

Typography by Stephanie Bart-Horvath   1 2 3 4 5 6 7 8 9 10 ✣ First Edition

MOONLIGHT
THE HALLOWEEN CAT

By Cynthia Rylant

Illustrated by Melissa Sweet

HarperCollinsPublishers

Moonlight loves the night.
It is her favorite time . . .

She walks, soft and black,
over the grass, along the fences,
through the trees.

Moonlight loves all the nights.
But Halloween is her favorite.

Things are a little different . . .

Pumpkins smile at her.

Straw laps welcome her.

And children are out.
Moonlight loves children.
She follows them, but they don't see her.
She is black, like the night.

On Halloween the moon is yellow and wide.
Moonlight sits in a tree and watches it.

Very late, the owls fly.
Moonlight watches them.

And sometimes, there's a rabbit.

Moonlight walks the night.
She sees lights going off in the houses.
Now only pumpkins will shine.

She sees raccoons on porches.

She sees stars in the pond.

She sees a dog in its warm little bed.

Moonlight is a Halloween cat.
It is her favorite night of all.

The pumpkins smile.

The stars shine.

And someone has dropped a candy.
A treat for a Halloween cat!